How HIGH is the

By Tony Farmer
Illustrated by Lynne Farmer

Child's Play (International) Ltd
Swindon   Bologna   New York
© M. Twinn 1991 ISBN 0-85953-517-7 Printed in Singapore
Library of Congress Number 91-19350
This impression 1993

One day, when Oswald was out for a walk,
He saw one of Mr Handley's wagons.

It was as tall as a house and painted bright red.
The truck towered high above Oswald's head.

Oswald wondered, **"Is a wagon as high as the moon?"**

Out of the cab stepped Oswald's friend, Gilpin Bland.
He was holding a spanner in his right hand.

Oswald asked him, **"Is your wagon as high as the moon?"**

Gilpin smiled and looked up at the sky.

"No, no, Oswald. The moon is ever so high!"

Oswald walked on, until he came to a hole.
In it, some workmen were planting a pole.

Oswald thought,
"This pole might be as high as the moon."

Sitting nearby was old Mrs Mole.
Her shiny coat was as black as coal.
Oswald asked her, **"Is this pole as high as the moon?"**

Mrs Mole brushed some dirt from her bright flowered skirt.
And she sighed a sad sigh, as she made her reply.

**"Why, Oswald, I have never seen the moon floating by.
For my poor little eyes, it is much too high!"**

Oswald continued his walk through the glade.
He came to an oak tree and sat in its shade.

On a branch of the tree sat Merlin the owl.
He had just had a bath and was wrapped in a towel.

Oswald asked, **"Is this tree as high as the moon?"**

The owl gave a hoot and blinked an eye.
Then he cocked back his head and stared up at the sky.

**"No, Oswald. My eyesight is good.
And I have seen nothing as high as the moon
in the whole of this wood."**

Around the next bend, Oswald heard a bump,
As a big red balloon came to earth with a thump.
Then two cheeky monkeys tied its rope to a stump.

Oswald said, **"Sirs, you made me jump! Can your balloon fly as high as the moon?"**

The monkey explorers travel far and wide.
Their balloon sails high over the countryside.

They said, **"Our balloon can touch the sky. But the moon is higher than we can fly!"**

Oswald came to a barn, built high on a mound.
He waited and listened, but he couldn't hear a sound.
So he knocked on the door, and to his surprise,
Out came a cow of enormous size.

Oswald looked up and asked,
   "Is your barn as high as the moon?"

The cow was wearing a bright blue tie.
She had a black patch over one eye.
She yawned at Oswald, then mooed with a sigh,

"No, dear Oswald. The moon is high!"

Oswald saw a kite, floating in the breeze,
Swooping and looping high over the trees.
Oswald followed the string and, where it came down,
Hanging on tight, was Charlie, the clown.

Oswald asked,
"Charlie, can your kite fly as high as the moon?"

Charlie answered,
"I think it might, though I never fly my kite at night.
I like to watch the moon in the sky.
But I don't have enough string to reach so high!"

When Oswald arrived at the church on the hill,
The whole of the town lay quiet and still.

From his nest in the spire, with a cry of alarm,
A raven flew down and perched on Oswald's arm.

Oswald asked, **"Raven, is this spire as high as the moon?"**

The raven flapped his great wings and opened his beak.
In a solemn voice, he began to speak.

**"Although it is reached by sweet songs from the choir,
To tell you the truth, the moon is far higher than the spire."**

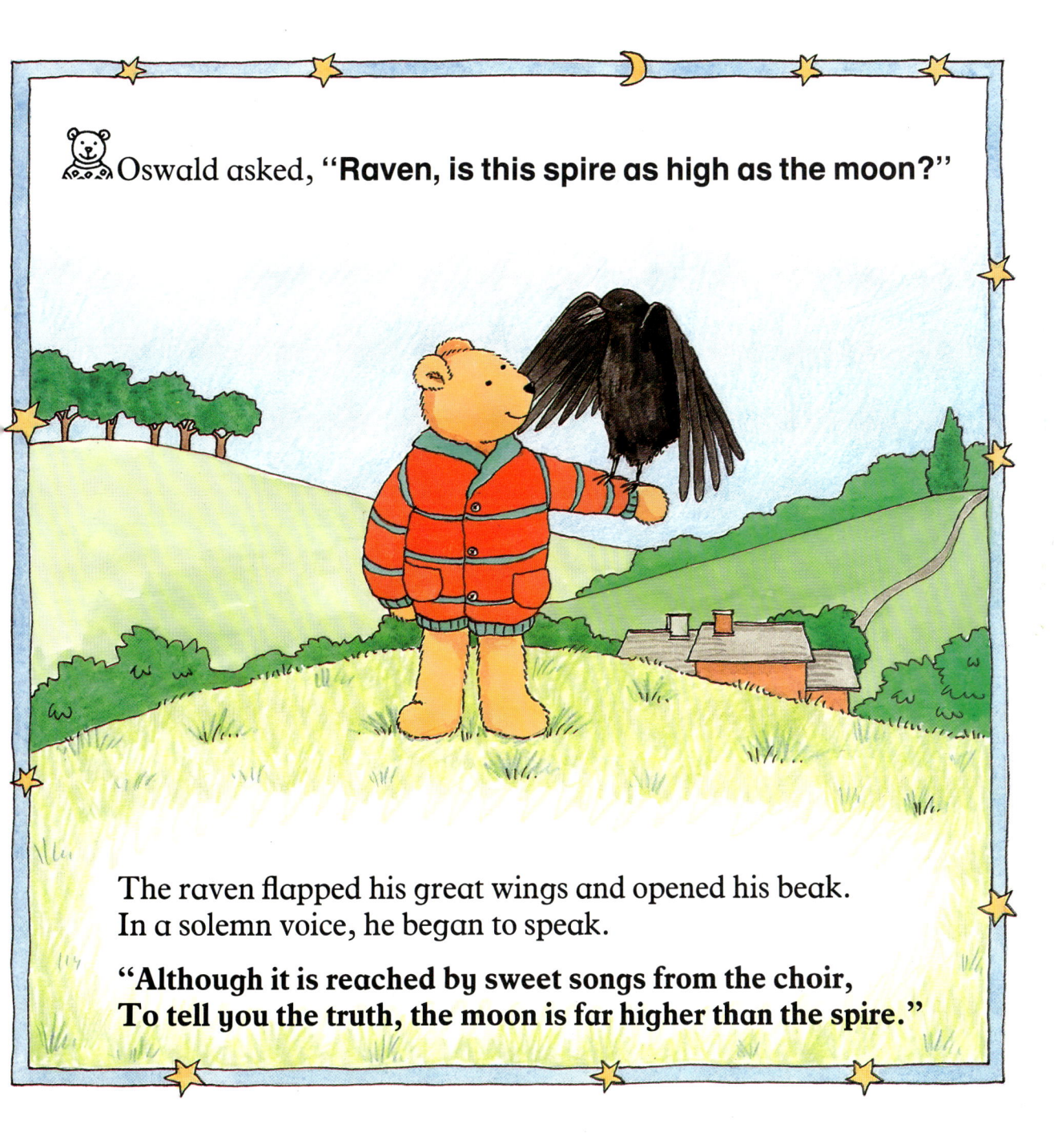

It was growing dark, much too late to be out.
"**Help! I am lost!**" Oswald started to shout.

Then the moon appeared, all silver and white,
Bathing the world in its magical light.

Oswald took out a toy from his cardigan pocket.
It was one he liked best, a little toy rocket.

In the light of the moon, to Oswald's surprise,
It slowly began to grow in size.

Oswald switched on the motor and clambered on board.
He started the engine by pulling a cord.

The rocket roared off, straight to the moon.
"**At this speed,**" laughed Oswald, "**we'll be there soon.**"

The Man in the Moon was conducting his band.
When the rocket landed, he shook Oswald's hand.

Then Oswald said, **"Sir, how do you do?
There is one question, which I want to ask you.
How high is the moon?"**

The old man sat Oswald upon his toe,
And rocked him gently to and fro.

"Hold tight, little bear, and look down below!"

So, Oswald looked down as far as he could,
Till he saw the faint lights of his town by the wood.

The old man told Oswald about the moon.

**"It circles the earth like a great balloon.
It brightens the darkest sky at night.
When you look up from earth, it's a wonderful sight."**

"It is as high from the earth, as the earth from the moon.
Now, promise me, Oswald, to come again soon.
For now it is time to say goodbye.
It is long past your bedtime. You really must fly."

Oswald said, "**Thank you. You have taught me to see, How high is a matter of degree.**"

Then, thinking of supper and the friends in his town, Oswald climbed on his rocket and flew it back down.

Later that night,
As he lay in his bed,
With extra pillows
To prop up his head,
Oswald gazed at the moon . . .

. . . and let out a deep sigh.

"Nothing at all in this world is so high.

**Though the moon is nearer than any star,
Only one bear has travelled so far."**